A FOOL FOR Christmas

· ·

A TALE BY ALLAN GURGANUS

HORSE & BUGGY PRESS

IN ASSOCIATION WITH DUKE UNIVERSITY LIBRARIES

DISTRIBUTED BY DUKE UNIVERSITY PRESS

BUY ME?

**ELL, welcome to my mall, stranger.**
And "Merry, merry" back at you. You just come
in off the highway? This ice is scary, idn't it?
They say traffic's backed up nearbout to Charlotte.

Saving this stool?   *Well, aren't you nice.*

Me, I'm Vernon Ricketts and I manage our Fin, Fur and Fun franchise.
Third-busiest pet store in eastern North Carolina, so they tell me.

Yep, finally closed, Christmas Eve. Not to brag, but my staff and me
today? We "moved" more animals than ole Noah ever did. And while
each of my pups and kittens goes speeding home toward sleeping kids?
Mr. Manager has swung in here for a big old final drink.

Bet you're glad you're off that Interstate. Lucky you found our
county's one place still open, it being a holiday after one A.M . . .

Kirsten runs this bar; there she is yonder. Still beautiful, 'm I right?
We went through school together, her and me. Survived the same crazed
Pentecostal church. Had our own Bibles, our own tambourines. Kirsten's
husband left her flat with two young boys.

Ran off with his horseback-riding teacher, a ex-Marine like him.
Shocker. Oh but Kirsten dealt with it, has got a lot of spirit. And, for
us mall-insiders, tonight only, she always makes personal eggnog.

Family recipe, grates her own nutmeg,

brings in the home-blender,

everything.

Yo, Kirst-en! Looking fine in that red ermine-lined mini. How those twins? We'll need a couple your famous eggnogs, me and my new pal here.

You'll see, they're super-tasty. I keep trying to "reduce" . . . but hey, man, it's Christmas Eve.

Tonight is even more than the start of a whole day-off for Vernon here, it's secretly my anniversary. I can't help remembering, with us in the middle of a blizzard and all. Yeah, this same second be 'xactly one year ago, in my exceptional pet shop through that very security screen, I DID something. Still don't know how, nor why a certain person trusted me to help with it. Got us both into newspapers, the Charlotte one plus Raleigh's. But, along with being **exceptional** store-publicity, turned out to be the best darn thing that ever grabbed me. Finest gift a woman ever give me. And right here at the holidays. Even before it happened, I was a fool for Christmas.

Well, imagine me now.

I ask you, is that eggnog or is that not eggnog?
Kirsten, keep 'em coming, honey. Merry merry.

First time I seen the girl that changed me so majorly, poor thing was already being hounded. We do got a "No Vagrant" policy at this shop-ping center. Never was enforced. Not till Vanderlip stepped in as Mall Manager. He was soon all over our drifters, skate-boarders, even the rich old men nodding off while wives tried on every shoe in each store.

Vanderlip is one strange bird. Seems there's lots of the military-minded taking charge these days. He come up hard, like I did. Attending night-school after having two kids while working three jobs — you got to respect that type-drive in a family man. Big church-goer,

too. Big Baptist. Vanderlip witnesses for Christ, right at the urinal, feeling sure you'll stand exactly *there* at least till either you finish or *he* does. But seems-like the better Vanderlip does in life, the harder he is on those he passed during his scrappy climb clear up to "MALL MANAGER."

Man ain't that old but he's always acted sixty-five, born taking names. Too proud of being in charge. Even of a mall like ours, with just three the fountains working and no Restoration Hardware.

F irst we thought he'd be **GOOD** for the place. Didn't he bring in bigger palm trees? Didn't he release dozens of my shop's largest goldfish into reflecting pools? (Till the tossed pennies or the chlorine got them, one.) Was then Vanderlip caught a retired couple pocketing three-for-a-buck canned tuna at Dollar General. He marches them, sobbing, into the backroom he's labeled "De-Programming."

Thirty minutes later, old guy comes out of there . . . on a stretcher. Heart attack. Thin line between "background check" and "torture." Us merchants we'd first nicknamed Vanderlip "The Enforcer."

By now? He's "Terminator."

But yes, a new girl was seen on the mall. "Terminator" Vanderlip spotted her first. Oh, she tried blending in with other pretties that age. She would settle, keeping her back to our usual standout blondes monop-olizing the popular benches fountain-side. Young gals are always dabbing glitter make-up onto each other, then taking cell phone snaps of their new navel rings, sending these to lucky farm-boys out in the county.

But this recent gal wore just an old sailor's peacoat sizes too big. Had limp brown hair all down in her face. Plastic barrettes pushed bangs into being the little awning letting her hide in plain sight.

Prettier girls, bare-midriffs, migrate like birds around our Grand Concourse. All at once they'll rush like mad to avoid *or attract* some clump of boys just arrived.

I saw this darker new child follow that crowd, but only at a distance, just so's she'd fade in a little better. They ignored her. She acted like she didn't notice being snubbed. But at that age that's all you notice.

Me, I noticed. While settling Siamese kittens into our cedared bay-windows, I wondered why this one gal, of all fifteen hundred mall-visitors per-day, should catch my interest. Or my pity maybe?

I guess she was not what you'd call real attractive, only tiny, you know. Small in a way that frog-gigs the hearts of big ole fellows like me. She kept to herself. She fell somewhere betwixt twelve and seventeen; she fell between looking not too   interested and completely . . . lost.

Why **her?** Well, you know how in your smartphone's photo files, among all the snaps you took of your smiling friends and new real-leather furniture, there'll be some mess-up shots?

Maybe sky, some jet-trail and two flying birds, or even your own knee shown against the red steering wheel? What's odd, you flip right past the good pictures and stare longest at the ones gone somewhat wrong. It's *those* ones make you think, "Hell, I could be a pho-**tog**-rapher!"

She was like that. Off to one side, a throwaway, kind of nifty but nearbout by acci-dent.

Right off I seen she was clever.

Never settling real long in one place.

Avoiding Vanderlip's catching steady sight of her.

Carrying a different store's bag each day.

Always chatting into her cell phone, body turned in odd directions, hunting privacy. But "Terminator" was right there behind the new palm tree, talking into his wristwatch. With his nose for sin, Vanderlip guessed her story long before I did.

Man walks in short steps so he always seems real busy, busy. Never without the tie; its knot big as a thermos. And since 9-11 and these mall shootings every week, two lapel pins, right and left, the American flag opposite one white enameled cross. Wears them like personal ID.

J UST AFTER EACH THANKSGIVING, Vanderlip has signs hung across our mall's four sides, "Jesus IS the Reason for the Season" and — under that — in small print, "and happy hanuka." Spelled "Hanukkah" wrong; some say on purpose. His own church-choir has been singing carols here every Tuesday–Thursday since Halloween.

My new favorite she now fetched up only on the rainy coldest days. Seemed she was saving back our shelter for when she'd need it most. Never really stepped into *my* shop. But, like everybody, she would gather before our snow-sprayed windows full of wriggling pups all wearing red bows. I'd see her sort of grinning then. I willed her to visit Vernon's menagerie. I thought, "Out yonder, hungry, stands somebody's daughter." I imagined her as being mine, then shuddered. I felt *more* scared for her after that.

So, was three weeks before last Christmas, I seen something I wasn't supposed to. That sweet sad mouse-girl steps into the Ladies, leaves her cell phone on one fountain-side bench. Well, I figure here's Vernon's chance to be a hero, see? So I rush out to save the cell she's been chatting into constant for these three weeks, especially when "Terminator's" staring.

But hers? it's just a toy. For kids. From Dollar General. Black block of wood, cheap decal sticky on its front.

So lightweight I all but dropped it. I set it down real quick and run off, huffing. I figure: Let her keep her secrets till she can't.

Thanks for the fresh eggnog, Kirsten. Each glass a meal in itself, huh?
Look, do I got foam on my chin?   Thanks

Girl ate alone in our International Food Court. I saw how sly she worked that place. She'd make a off-to-one-side meal out of dispenser ketchup, leftover croutons, hot water. She'd garnish this with lemon wedges then a lil Parmesan from Mamma Mia's. Out of a bin, dainty, she'd lift one large soda cup, wash it good at our water fountain then drink Classic Coke all day. One time I saw her stash her cup up high on a ledge so's Vanderlip's over-busy cleanup-crew wouldn't snag it. Girl's jacket hikes up and underneath, I see: she's like ten months pregnant. White belly squared-off to where it seems she's swallowed a twelve-pound dice.

What next? The shopper I really like best now, the one I find I'm waiting to see daily? Pregnant, 'bout fourteen. Just Vernon's luck.

Me, see, I basically — even romance-wise — I run Animal Rescue. Even while retailing brand-new creatures, I am really running a orphanage. It's the same, even on blind dates, which my dates mostly are. I guess gals don't like it when you act real **kind** to them.

I try holding back and sounding semi-mean. But look at me. I am, on sight, a softie. And they guess. Reckon nobody's perfect.

I think I do pretty good for a GED-type person. Got me the vintage Camaro, 'SS-3838, stroke four-speed, cherry red. My condo's half paid-off, real-leather sectionals "Merlot-Maroon." Plus, before they closed, I had seen everything at Blockbuster twice, and not just

Tarantino, neither. I don't know why gals all feel there's too much
of me to be much of a catch.

But, Christmas-week coming in hard, we got us a bad ice storm.
Like tonight's. Driving slow to work, I think, "Good. She'll be in easy
sight today." Does show up, round noon. I notice orange mud is caked
knee-high on her jeans. I guess she's not used to being this dirty.
You can tell from how she moves . . . her boots are soaked.

M Y RUNAWAY is still too used to regular home bubble-
baths, see. Nobody can live anymore at ease in ditches
and out in the woods. Even Pioneers, you wonder
how they managed. And her "with child"! to use Bible talk. Coat collar
up, she looks all shivery, talking her grown-up secrets into a dollar toy.

So, well, I, I carry out our blondest possible cocker puppy, big
plaid taffeta bow round its neck, naturally. Hold it down to where
she slumps beside the Ann Taylor bag fooling absolutely nobody.
Meanwhile Vanderlip stands describing her into a walkie-talkie lots
more real than her phone.

I go, "Hi. I'm Vernon? in charge of that there pet-store? Would you mind picking up a little change for sitting out here holding, like, the cutest dog in the whole mall? Because I been looking somebody to demonstrate this animal for potential buyers. When folks stop and pat young Butterbean here — (meet "Butterbean") — you just refer said customers to my shop yonder. — Pretty easy money. And I think that you are just the charming gal, the very mall-regular, to put this over."

She finally whispers but right toward our pup's brown eyes, "This one's such a young one, ain't it?" Gal holds that lickin pup so close its nose is hid under her hairdo. But from certain shoulder motions, I can tell she's crying.

Then I say, "Look. I am going to laugh 'cause Security is, like, so onto you. I'm about to pretend you're funny and we're friends already." I do that then, you know, I chuckle. People expect that from guys my jolly Santa size. But under my breath like, I start telling her:

I know her cell phone is a block of pinewood, know she's crying 'cause this here's a baby dog and she is toting another baby all over creation and my mall. I add as how I'd like to help if I can. Especially seeing how it's the holidays and all. I say if she does carry Butterbean clear from Penney's down to our Dillard's even a couple-three times, expect to meet me at Chung-King Express around two for her free demonstrator's lunch, okay? I warn her, I go, "Don't you cry now. You get me started, there's no stopping it. Some say I'm a fool for Christmas. Some say just a fool. — But don't be feeling mopey and too bad, child. Cause Vernon, he knows your story now."

Well, at the Food Court, over fried dumplings and Butterbean, I ask what I usually ask my dates: who her kid's real father is. Holding the pup between us, this girl speaks extra soft. I tilt nearer to hear her go, "He's Warren. Just started his third tour o' Afghanistan. He's in Bravo Company. They got him carrying his rifle through a city made out of clay like flowerpots and Warren he's clearing it one apartment at a time. Says he never knows what he'll find from door to door. There's days he says he cannot catch his breath. First tour, him and his buddy had to make theirselves extra armor out of parts of things like old 'frigerators.

"But Warren swears every door he opens is one less any other American boy or girl will have to. He's lost his two best friends there. Soon as he makes a friend, says they get killed.

Warren **swears** he won't be shot,

       says *third* tour's the charm.

       Says a person just knows these things.

Three's always been my lucky number! 'Warren' doesn't sound like a name that's too exciting but he is. Before tour three, I wondered what I could do to **help** him back here. Didn't want the boy to just get blown up like them others. I hated he would have nothing left to show for even being on Earth. Figured he deserves at least a Junior.

"Oh Warren can play three instruments and talk about can sing! When he gets through this tour, he is going to Nashville to produce CDs that are half-rap, half-country. It's new. He'll be the biggest thing in music since the King, m' Warren. Having his son was all my idea. He don't even know about my projeck. See, I stuck one of my barrette-wires through all our protections. My Dad he preaches part-time? And he told me if I ever got in the family way not to even bother coming home. So, I left before I showed any. Warren he give me 1500 dollars.

"Still got most of it.   — This Chinese egg roll, I would say, is excellent."

I see Vanderlip about to head our way. He will ask her if she's had a complete Browse-and-Buy Mall holiday experience, and what have been her purchases these last few weeks? Receipts, please.

So, just to talk, I start quizzing her about where she lives. Then she gets all stiff, speaks real cold into her fortune cookie, "North of here. With my Aunt, why?" I thought, "Yeah, north of our parking lot, in woods with more ants than *one*, probably." So when Mr. Mall Manager does bob up, I explain she has this dog out on approval. A trusted regular.

"Merry Christmas," she smiles up to Vanderlip and he just looks her over.

W ITH EIGHT DAYS TILL YULETIDE PROPER, she finally steps to the back of my shop, bringing Butterbean in from their latest demonstration tour.

Before I even see the girl, there comes this hush. Now, my animals don't usually react to a customer one-way-the-other. Maybe her being so pregnant struck them? Or her quiet habit of taking not one thing for granted. Even two full-grown jumpy Maine Coon Cats shift forward in their cages.

My all-time smartest African gray parrot says in a Vernon-like voice that cracks up our beauticians next-door, "Eww, who did that to your HAIR?" Well, hearing, she laughs like a kid then. Under bangs, I see her teeth. She shows part of one great eye, brown.

Soon I had her helping my trusted assistant-manager LaTonya do preliminary grooming. I leave the big Labs and shepherds for our sturdy after-high-school boys. One thing is, I have a top-notch staff.

Listen, you cannot sell a hundred and nineteen holiday pups plus eighty-two kittens without having you some able helpers, are you kidding?

I liked seeing our new girl use the blow-dryer on a apricot toy poodle. She looked totally into it, finally training for something, you know.

During one of her many bathroom trips, LaTonya and I found the wallet in her peacoat, us scouting for some family phone number. But she'd smartly marked the contact-info off of everything — *that* determined to do all this alone. I noticed she was down to ninety nine dollars, mostly ones and fives. Like me, LaTonya had already offered her a place to stay but our little girl she was too proud. Kept talking about her being a guest of that fancy Aunt of hers. Well, to judge from muddy boots, that aunt must've lived in a cave.

Was three days before Christmas we had downpours, sleet, high winds, and she goes missing. Naturally I'm worried sick. Already I am picturing this pale gal, dead in a ditch beside her new baby. Used to, I'd go crazy waiting for my Mom and Grandma to get home from the box factory. Now I had LaTonya checking three times daily all Ladies Rooms mall-wide.

So that night right after work, I aim my Camaro out toward our lot's far north corner. Leave my brights on, whip out my phone's flashlight app, go squishing through puddles.

I aim toward huge walk-in concrete pipes, all lined up to be part of that new Target going in next door. They been dropped in among our last few sassafras and sweet-gum trees, all that's left of old American woods hereabouts.

The sky, from low clouds and strip-mall signs, shows ox-blood-red this time the night. My breath clouds. Muzak carols drift clear out here, words and everything, "How still we see thee lie, above thy dark and dreamless streets, the silent stars go by . . . " But, funny, my mall, from this back-dumpster-angle tonight looks almost ugly. That's from my missing her, from my worry, I reckon.

Then, before one big pipe, I see flooring made of scrap plywood, laid just so. Bricks circle a cold campfire. Inside that four-foot-pipe, my flashlight finds garbage bags stuffed with leaves for bedding. Two empty cans of Old Milwaukee. And, hooked to one wall, a little round hand-mirror.

Hanging onto it, I see an old Smurf doll with all of one girl's pink barrettes clipped into that toy's orange hair. Well, that tore me up.

I don't know.

People are so **brave,** you know?

I HEAR ANOTHER BODY'S SHOES slushing the dark nearby and Vernon jumps like from a horror movie but calling to her, crying almost, "That you, babe? Say you're safe." And here stands Vanderlip.

Strange to find him in his suit, snooping out this far. Sunset flashes his lapel pins red, with all the rest of him left dark. He's like, "So, Vernon, come out here after work, do ya? Get a little steam off? Girl that low, living back out here like some rat in a hole and you standing in front of her pipe. That's it, idn't it?"

Old as I am, being forty, you forget you can still feel shocked. But I have been living so far past such filthy thoughts as his, first I, I, I, didn't even understand him. Defending her, I knew I was going to say what I'd never dared speak before to any hall-monitor like him.

"Might could surprise you, Mr. Vanderlip, with your praying into our loudspeaker every morning for sales, with your church-choir handing out Sin leaflets noon and night, but there's still some good folks left on Earth. You feel s'fine about yourself you expect everything **but** good from others. There's way more sin in your mind than you'll find out here at the edge, where most people just try and live. She's one the good ones, sir. She's your daughter Tammy's age and no worse.

    "You invent an enemy a day. That's your caffeine that wakes you up. The others ain't enemies at first. But they *start* being, once you treat them like 'at. Her boyfriend's off serving in Afghanistan, sir. I ain't ever been out here before tonight. It's that she's missing. How'd you even know about her camp?"

"Security reconnaissance. She's been building off-site fires, code violation. Why? What'd you do with her body, Vernon? You're just the type. I know you've been slipping her the odd tenner. I have my sources. Funny, when I started here as Manager? You struck me as a real retail-leader, Verne. You knew how to mix up the big and little breeds of pups, Great Danes beside Chihuahuas all wearing Easter Bunny ears in one Old English window. And you got **points** with me for that. Did. You could always stop thirty customers dead in their tracks out front of your shop. Sure, you need to drop about a hundred and fifty pounds. But, once that's done, you might could find a future even higher up in Management. Instead? you've got half the High School working for you where one qualified adult'd do. You overpay them out of your own pocket. And now you put that little skank on payroll right at Christmas?

    "God knows what other bagboys she's been kneeling in a pipe and doin' back here for pocket-change. Wise up, Vernon. She's carrying somebody else's load."

    I felt tempted to tell him about his daughter Tammy's reputation. I was about to sound off about what lessons Baby Jesus's stable taught, but I, I, I, just let it go. There is too much to explain to any man this sure he's the Baptist angel-grade of "good."

So finally, after her going missing three full days, come Christmas Eve closing time, I see the Terminator's Security Boys surround a small person at our Grand Concourse fountain.

LaTonya alerts me, "Verne, it her okay. She back, but she looking *real* shook." I rush out, tell them she's my niece and I'll handle my own family mess. Good thing Vanderlip was off chasing Dillard's formalwear shoplifters into "Day at the Beach Tanning Parlor." As I bend down to help, poor child says, "I hitched halfway home, but they're too churchy to take in no bad girl like me. This old lady outside Ahoskie picked me up, carried me to her house, but she kept trying and get in the bathtub with me. Vernon, it got to where it was almost kind of weird. But right along, I kept thinking I've just have to get back to Verne and them pups. — But, am *hurtin'* some."

She stares right up at me, her face dead-white, emergency. Then I see as how her jeans are soaked clear through; her waters had done broke. If I knew little, she knew less. At least I had the delivery of eight hundred pups and kittens under my belt. In the valley of the blind . . .

LaTonya, knowing my tendency with strays, tried to warn me. She stands behind the gal, shaking her head No. And I understand LaTonya's right. So I tell the child, "We need us a hospital, girl. This one's beyond even me, glad as I am you're home." Then that child sandwiches both her little paws around one of mine, man-sized. Gal says louder than ever she has spoke before, "Got no in-surance. My folks is probably already told the police I'm missing. Be a world of trouble if I step into a ER. I don't want to get you into no bad fix on my 'count. Us not being kin, doctors'd send you off anyways. But I couldn't stand for this to happen among strangers, Verne. Please. See? with Warren away, I done come clear back to **YOU** for this. Please — I'm strong."

Well, when somebody's chosen you, however much you might want Nine-one-one? you are, well, you're . . . chose.

So while Vanderlip is scaring naked folks in tanning beds, LaTonya and me get her back into our storeroom. A trail of water on linoleum.

Hiding from Security, LaTonya, a big CSI fan, mops up evidence. The DNA, whathaveyou, it all tells a story.

Right off, I run to my beloved Internet. Vernon Googles keywords "Baby," "Human," "Delivery of." Kept the printout folded in my back-pocket all that busy day.

Things stayed pretty hectic sales-wise it being Christmas Eve and ever-thing. We do 39.3 percent of our business after Thanksgiving. Yes, Vanderlip goes rushing everywhere, grilling everybody about where she's got to.

Man never knew we'd lock her safe back here with us, behind stacked bags of every Hartz Mountain Canary product.

So. — So, yeah, it was right at a year ago tonight, about this exact same minute, see? I move my Camaro clear down to the Hardee's lot toward Old Raleigh Road, then hiked back, huffing. If Vanderlip had seen my '67 "cherry-red" nearby, he'd of barged into my shop with cops, social services and his own crazed finger-wagging preacher probably.

For once, I lock my store from inside. Turned out all the lights except aquariums.' Now, I tell you, the sounds of a pet shop is easier to notice in the dark.   Fish tanks' bubbling becomes

          like ticking clocks,   a sweet background   calming. Lights off, you can even hear our reptiles move their own sand. Around one A.M., her and me perked up and felt a bit afraid when the mall's great outside metal doors slammed shut then echoed everywhere like inside a whole castle.

My girl kept trying not to scream. By then her jeans were off and I had our store's every space heater putting pink light to all the sides of her. I tell her, "Just us chickens. Don't hold back none now." Well, then she flat lets rip.

Shrieks echo across a sleeping mall, bouncing off each glassy storefront. This place will feel forever more alive for that, for me.

She screams in waves and rows, and I called down into the heat from her breath and body, a little stove. I found a way to coach her, "We're getting there! You can! You can! You are, girl!" I see now — every creature must be valuable if each birth takes this much work.

I T WAS NOT NO HOLIDAY NIGHT OFF. But I guess I might call this the most testing, flattering thing that's ever once been asked of ole Vernon here. To be so trusted, and on Christmas Eve and hid in with her among our animals!

Then it got so sudden, and even the top of the head looked like a human head, because it was, it was one. Somehow it got out whole, we got it out. Amazing that she'd hung around my mall and drew me a bit forward, found me. I cut the cord with my highest-end dog nail-clippers (but brand-new, plus sterilized). Amazing that, when the time was right, she had hitched clear back to be with me here, and that I *could* get down there and pull and coax and catch it — then hold its ankles up like it was some lizardy pet but slapping into it the air that made it go human.

I had saved back one tartan-plaid Burberry cashmere dog jacket, softest thing in the store beside birds, and our most expensive. I wrapped her child in that and laid it in the mother's arms.

By the end, she says, small, but meaning it — "This here's the first *real* thing I ever done, and you was with me ever' step, sweet Verne."

I goes just, "Thanks."

Well, it was a male one — I mean, it was a boy.

Oh, he was a pretty little thing. Black hair spread out like damp feathers. But of course I would call him pretty. I would, as his — whatever — as her substitute, as at least a fairly good pet store manager. Then I did something foolish, but it felt great. I let out all the puppies and kittens, ones that had not been sold in time? And it did not take them long to drift back here and find where all this new mewing was coming from. My best African gray flew over to perch on a pegboard partition and look down at her and the babe and asked, "Eww, what did they do to your *hair*!" Well, she cracked up.

Y EAH, WAS JUST LAST CHRISTMAS EVE, lit by saltwater tanks, behind the staff lounge in my dark belov-ed pet store, in a mall with just us three, and other animals surrounding us, locked up tight from the outside in, together.

The baby dogs and cats could smell her built-up milk, hoping it would fountain out soon, first real mother's milk. And the excitement of her scent and the blood and this slick new little life, it made them crazy with the kind of joy and jumpiness I'd never seen, not in all my years of retail here.

Of course, I couldn't keep her and him hiding in my storeroom forever. Even I knew that. And she didn't think it right, her staying long at my place without us being married or nothing. Oh I understood. But she'd have forever been safer-than-safe living life with Vernon here. Whatever she wanted, I'd of dealt with it, really. Even being an ample person, what with eleven hundred square feet, I had plenty of room for little folks like them.

Finally, I did get the parents' phone number out of her. Called them. Told them she'd had a son, named both for Warren and for her father, which would make that boy the fourth. And there came a stillness and the mother finally said, "How are they?"

I drove them both to the Raleigh airport in my Camaro, waxed perfect. I got as near the gate as the person without a ticket *can* go nowdays. And, just before the X-ray machine, she turns back, tells me she will make "Vernon" an extra middle name of his, which was . . . quite the Christmas gift.

Sometimes her mom still sends me pictures of this ideal baby on the Web.   I sure save every attachment.

Just did what anybody would have, really. Still, I've taken his best baby picture and — well, he's my screen-saver now.

Oh, man. Sorry. Blubbering here. Can be such a pushover. And a big ol' boy like me, too.

But hey, this time the year, could be — getting a little Sentimental's legal, right? You been s' nice to talk to, really. Yeah, well that was last December twenty-fourth. And, I guess I'd have to say it was — of all Vernon's Christmases — his most — *per*-sonal.

You got to get on the road, I see that in your face. . . .

Kirsten, precious, can I settle up the tab for me and my newest friend here? You kept us real well-supplied.

What? No, Kirsten. Not this many, not for free! Naw, Vernon cannot "accept." You give others way too much, girl.— Well, but . . . well, just looks like I'm going to have to sneak you and your twins something extra up ahead. Their birthday's March eleventh, I believe?

Guess I'd best be speeding home, too. Snooze me fourteen hours straight. Holiday emotions this big, they wear out even a plus-size person. Hey, good luck on that highway, getting where your folks're all expecting you tomorrow.

Imagine Kirsten not letting me pay for any of our many eggnogs! Old family recipe, made with hand-grated nutmeg in her own home-blender.

Oh, I know folks say I tend to be a fool for Christmas. But, I swear, once a year, maybe we should all just go ahead and admit it . . .

. . . Ain't people wonderful!

The Tale Behind The Tale ALLAN GURGANUS

Once a story breathes itself alive, its genesis grows harder to trace.
But this one's infancy, I remember:

*In 2004, I got a phone call from NPR's "All Things Considered." Would I write
a story then read it on-air Christmas Eve? I'd have two weeks to complete and
record it. Like many people, I just dread deadlines. But this challenge seemed
worthwhile. I knew that my attempt — acknowledging a Christian holiday
— must speak to Muslims, agnostics, children, everybody. I hoped to make it
not just a stylish short story but a genuine tale. Since I was expected to perform
it aloud, my narrator should probably be male. I wanted the action to be
contemporary. Maybe some lesser mall might make a good setting.*

    *Certain adults imagine owning a cool bar like Rick's American Café.
Since childhood, I've fantasized about a pet shop. Such a mall store's staff chang-
ing room might prove the coziest spot to spend some lonesome Christmas Eve.
The story began to whisper itself alive aloud.*

    *Who might run such a North Carolina pet shop? Would he be grouchy,
compassionate, both? An unemployable academic dropout or some self-made
GED entrepreneur? Detectives find a crime then follow it in reverse. Storytellers
instigate acts; and if those don't work, they lob others.*

    *To hatch a tale worthy of "All Things Considered's" twelve million listeners
at six p.m. on Christmas Eve — I must rearrange my next two weeks. I'd gladly
sacrifice sleep. I vowed to bail on any social occasion not a best friend's funeral.
I stockpiled Greek yogurt and French roast. In this way, through interchange-
able dawns and sunsets, Vernon Ricketts's comfy pet store became my very own
hamster wheel.*

*It was three years after the World Trade Center towers fell. Persons in control
of North America's public-spaces had hardened their policing tactics. Airport
security now required humiliating shoe-removal. Even managers of Carolina*

malls felt underdressed if they left home without lapel pins representing both church and state. To first hear Vernon, I had to map those forces daily arrayed against his big heart. Who in authority most objected to Verne's bending rules to protect his favorite underdogs? Fiction thrives on opposition. Vernon's habitual charities needed some strong countervailing force. Once "Terminator" Vanderlip appeared, the narrative's energy quickened.

Malls are often considered ugly, soulless places. But I recall being at one just before its shops opened. I noticed certain lab-coated beauticians gathered before the hardware establishment next door, flirting with its aproned clerks. A hundred years ago this would've happened on some pretty village green. I decided the luckiest malls must have a self-selected den mother — someone who remembers janitorial birthdays, someone who keeps track of this week's loitering runaways.

I soon felt myself listening out for (then inventing) one such caretaker. He'd be his mall's bard, host, registrar. These were unsalaried positions, jobs largely unacknowledged even by him. I named him "Vernon" (as a bow to the vernal nature of a man who loves animals, even the baffling human kind). To complicate his optimism I cited his impoverished boyhood: I made him a "Ricketts." This referenced a bone-softening childhood disease linked to malnutrition.

Early in the writing, I determined to never give Vernon's fourteen-year-old waif a name. After all, wasn't she traveling with a self-defaced ID? Though this would call for many synonyms, I managed to keep her innocent of any legally binding middle-class name, even a first one. I also made her the age of Romeo's Juliet and of Mary, the mother of Christ. My goal all along had been to create a present-time nativity. This stable-menagerie would be stocked not with sheep and donkeys, but imported parrots, tropical fish. The illumination wouldn't be shepherds' torches but lighted aquariums. The newborn had to be male. Vernon would serve in the role of Joseph, that generous cuckold delivering a child he knows to be engendered by potent forces unknowable. "Someone else's load."

Channeling Vernon Ricketts, I read the tale to a few friends then recorded it. NPR added ambient barroom sounds meant to create an eggnog atmosphere. The response was positive. Tom Campbell, co-founder of the Regulator Bookshop in Durham, North Carolina, heard the Christmas Eve broadcast on his car radio. Like Vernon, Tom was bound home from a very long day's work. He asked if I might perform the tale at his store the following December. Fifteen years along, this reading has become a casual tradition. The shop's new ownership continues the holiday ritual, replete with cookies and mulled cider. After my offertory reading, our assembled faithful — using the excuse of Q and A — discuss the year behind us and the one ahead. Though we meet in a book store not a pet shop, its atmosphere seems to underwrite this story of renewal.

Over time, I have revised and slightly lengthened the tale. Of course, technology has changed everything in a decade and a half. Vernon's comments on photography were first based on his mall's One Hour Photo Processing Booth. The digital revolution demands certain constant upgrades. Though polished annually, my tale has gone unpublished till this edition. I'm glad to see my "Fool" so handsomely produced. I am grateful to Duke University Press and Dean Smith; to the Duke University Libraries' Deborah Jakubs and Sara Seten Berghausen; and to Horse & Buggy Press, its founder-designer, Dave Wofford.

The seasonal reading of this tale always stirs discussion about the state of our imperiled nation: how can we live lives like his — making virtue a daily possibility? Fictional though Vernon is, I'd like to believe that somewhere a shadow version of him — jovial with holiday eggnog — feels cheered knowing that his heroism is still celebrated, and on his favorite night of the Christian calendar.

Surely our beleaguered world needs less "Terminator" Vanderlip, more Vernon Ricketts.

When Duke acquired the literary archive of Allan Gurganus, we knew we were adding a remarkable body of work to our already strong collection of writers in the southern literary tradition. We knew scholars would be eager to delve into the early drafts and annotations, the fascinating research files, the extensive correspondence with fellow authors, the as-yet unfinished and unpublished works, and the evidence of Allan's other creative efforts—his visual art, his dramatic performances. But none of us realized that bringing Allan's archive here would bring his whole creative network of friends and fans along with him.

To celebrate the acquisition, we held a reading and reception in Allan's honor, hosted by the Libraries, the Center for Documentary Studies, and the Power Plant Gallery, which had organized a concurrent exhibit of Allan's remarkable artwork. The event was standing-room only, and attendees included students, community members, and artistic and literary luminaries from all over the Piedmont. The Regulator Bookshop pitched in, providing books for signing— and again this season provides the ritual venue for his reading of this very tale. It is fitting that Allan's Christmas story has come alive through the years in that sanctuary of and for readers. Allan, like Verne, can draw in even a stranger off the highway and make family of the unlikeliest of wanderers. Because, simply put, brothers and sisters, he can flat-out tell a story.

Now, once again, our relationship with Allan inspires us to enrich and expand our collaborations with community friends and fellow travelers. We are delighted to work with Horse & Buggy Press and Duke University Press to bring this first publication of "A Fool for Christmas" out of the archive and onto the page— a gift to us all.

DEBORAH JAKUBS
Rita DiGiallonardo Holloway University Librarian & Vice Provost for Library Affairs
Duke University Libraries

Hear where it all began! The 2004 broadcast of Allan reading the story is available on the National Public Radio website: https://tinyurl.com/foolforchristmas.

Allan Gurganus's fiction has been translated into sixteen languages. Books include *Oldest Living Confederate Widow Tells All*, *White People*, *Plays Well with Others*, *The Practical Heart*, and *Local Souls*. Gurganus's essays are seen on the Op-Ed page of the *New York Times* and in the *New York Review of Books*. He has been awarded a *Los Angeles Times* Book Prize, the American Academy of Arts and Letters Sue Kaufman Prize for best first novel, a Guggenheim Fellowship, a Lambda Literary Award, and a National Magazine Prize. Film adaptations of Gurganus's work have won four Emmys. A Fellow of the American Academy of Arts and Letters, Gurganus co-founded Writers Against Jesse Helms. His forthcoming book is *The Uncollected Stories of Allan Gurganus*.

Horse & Buggy Press has been designing and producing a wide range of books (over 150 of them) since 1996. The studio remains a solo endeavor with Dave Wofford manning the reins and remaining fully committed to the printed book as one of the most engaging, and long-lasting, cultural artifacts of our time. The 1997 illustrated edition of *It Had Wings* by Allan Gurganus is but one example of a book that won awards for both content and design. Recent projects include the hardcover children's book *Harpsichord Diaries* and *The Father Box*, a collaboration between writer John Lane and photographer Rob McDonald. Dave also curates a gallery, Horse & Buggy Press and Friends, which features work by dozens of established Southeastern artists and craftspersons. horseandbuggypress.com

This second printing of *A Fool for Christmas* was published in 2019. Allan was inspired to pick up pens and brushes to add illustrations to his never-quite-finished tale, and he and Dave worked collaboratively on the design over emails, phone calls, visits to Allan's house, and to the H&B studio in Durham. These chapbooks were printed and bound at Laser Image Printing in Durham.

ISBN 978–1–4780–0938–2
© Allan Gurganus

Horse & Buggy Press has been designing and producing a wide range of books (over 150 of them) since 1996. The studio remains a solo endeavor with Dave Wofford manning the reins and remaining fully committed to the printed book as one of the most engaging, and long-lasting, cultural artifacts of our time. The 1997 illustrated edition of *It Had Wings* by Allan Gurganus is but one example of a book that won awards for both content and design. Recent projects include the hardcover children's book *Harpsichord Diaries* and *The Father Box*, a collaboration between writer John Lane and photographer Rob McDonald. Dave also curates a gallery, Horse & Buggy Press and Friends, which features work by dozens of established Southeastern artists and craftspersons. horseandbuggypress.com

This second printing of *A Fool for Christmas* was published in 2019. Allan was inspired to pick up pens and brushes to add illustrations to his never-quite-finished tale, and he and Dave worked collaboratively on the design over emails, phone calls, visits to Allan's house, and to the H&B studio in Durham. These chapbooks were printed and bound at Laser Image Printing in Durham.

ISBN 978–1–4780–0938–2